THE
TURTLE BOY

KEALAN PATRICK BURKE

1

"All the world's a stage, Timmy Quinn, but it's not the only one..."

Delaware, Ohio
Friday, June 9th 1979

TIMMY, PETE'S HERE!" his mother called and Timmy scattered a wave of comics to the floor with his legs as he prepared himself for another day of summer. The bedsprings emitted a half-hearted squeak of protest as he sidestepped the comics with their colorful covers.

School had ended three days ago, the gates closing with a thunderous finality the children knew was the lowest form of deception. Even as they cast one last glance over their shoulders at the low, hulking building, the school had seemed smug and patient, knowing the children's leashes were not as long as they thought. But for now, there were endless months of mischief to be perpetrated, made all the more appealing by the lack of premeditation, the absence of design. The world was there to be investigated, shadowy corners and all.

Timmy hopped down the stairs, whistling a tune of his own making and beamed at his mother as she stepped aside, allowing the morning sunshine to barge into the hallway and set fire to the rusted head of his best friend.

"Hey Pete," he said as a matter of supervised ritual. Had his mother not been present, he would more likely have greeted his friend with a punch on the shoulder.

"Hey," the other boy replied, looking as if he had made a breakthrough in his struggle to fold in on himself. Pete Marshall was painfully thin and stark white with a spattering of freckles—the result of an unusual cocktail his parents had stirred of Maine and German blood—and terribly shy around anyone but Timmy. Though he'd always been an introverted kid, he'd become even more withdrawn after his mother passed away two summers ago. Now when Timmy spoke to him, he sometimes had to repeat himself until Pete realized he could not get away without answering. The boy was all angles, his head larger than any other part of his body, elbows and knees like pegs you could hang your coat from.

In contrast to Pete's shock of unruly red hair, Timmy was blond and tanned, even in winter when the bronze faded to a shadow of itself. The two of them were polar opposites but the best of friends, united by their unflagging interest in the unknown and the undiscovered.

According to Timmy's mother, it was going to get into the high nineties today, but the boys shrugged off her attempt to sell the idea of sun block and insect repellent. She clucked her tongue and closed the door on the sun, leaving them to wander across the yard toward the bleached white strip of gravel-studded road and the fields of ocean green beyond.

"So, what do you want to do today?" Timmy asked, kicking a stone he knew was big enough to hurt his toes if he got it at the wrong angle.

Pete shrugged and studied a curl of dried skin on his forefinger.

Timmy persisted. "Maybe we can finish digging that hole we started?"

Convinced there was a mass of undiscovered treasure lying somewhere beneath Mr. Patterson's old overgrown green bean field, the two boys had borrowed some shovels from Pete's garage and dug a hole until the earth changed color from dark brown to a Martian red. Then a storm had come and filled the hole with brackish water, quashing any notions they had about trying to find the rest of what had undoubtedly been the remnants of a meteor.

"Nah," Peter said quietly. "It was a stupid hole anyway."

"Why was it stupid?" The last word felt odd as it slipped from Timmy's mouth. In his house, "stupid" ranked right up there with "ass" as words guaranteed to get you in trouble if uttered aloud.

"It just was."

"I thought it was pretty neat. Especially the chunks of meteor. I bet there was a whole lotta space rock under that field. Probably the bones of old aliens too."

"My dad said it was just clay."

Timmy looked at him, his enthusiasm readying itself atop the downward slope to disappointment. "What was clay?"

Pete shrugged again, as if all this was something Timmy should have known. "The red stuff. It was just old dirt. My dad said it gets like that when it's far enough down."

"Oh. Well it *could* have been space rock."

A mild breeze swirled the dust around their feet as they left the cool grass and stepped on to the gravel. Although this path had been there for as long as they could remember, it had only recently become a conveyor belt for the trucks and bulldozers which had set up shop off beyond the tree line where new houses were swallowing up the old corn field. It saddened Timmy to see it. Though young, he could still remember his father carrying him on his shoulders through endless fields of gold, now replaced by the skeletons of houses awaiting skin.

"How 'bout we go watch the trains then?"

Pete looked at him, irritated. "You know I'm not allowed."

"I don't mean on the tracks. Just near them, where we can see the trains."

"No, if my dad found out, he'd kill me."

"How would he know?"

"He just would. He always knows."

Timmy sighed and kicked the rock back into the grass, where it vanished. He immediately began searching for another one. As they passed beneath the shade of a mulberry tree, purple stains in the dirt all that remained of the first fallen fruit, he shook his head, face grim.

"I wish that kid hadn't been killed up there."

Pete's eyes widened and he looked from Timmy to where the dirt road curved away from them along Myers Pond until it changed into the overgrown path to the tracks.

The summer before, thirteen-year-old Lena Richards and her younger brother Daniel had been riding their dirt bikes in the cornfield on the other side of the rails. When a freight train came rumbling through, Danny had thought it a great idea to ride along beside it in the high grass next to the tracks and despite Lena's protests, had done that very thing. Lena, thinking her brother would be safer if she followed, raced up behind him. Blasted by the displaced air of the train, Danny lost control of his bike and fell. Lena, following too close behind and going much faster than she realized to keep the pace, couldn't brake in time. The vacuum wrenched them off their bikes. Danny was sucked under the roaring train. Lena survived, but without her legs.

Or so the story went, but they believed it. The older kids said it was true.

As a result, Timmy and Pete and all the neighborhood kids were now forbidden to venture anywhere near the tracks. Even if they decided to ignore their parents, a funny looking car with no tires rode the rails these days, yellow beacon flashing in silent warning to the adventurous.

"They were stupid to ride that close to the train anyway," Pete said glumly, obviously still pining for their days of rail walking.

"Naw. It sounds cool to do something like that. Apart from, you know...the *dying* part an' all."

"Yeah well, we can't get close enough to watch the trains, so forget it."

"Well then you come up with something to do, Einstein."

Pete slumped, the burden of choice settling heavily on his shoulders. Beads of sweat glistened on his pale forehead as he squinted up at the sun. To their left, blank-faced white houses stood facing each other, their windows glaring eyes issuing silent challenges they would never have the animation to pursue. To the right, hedges reared high, the tangles of weeds and switch grass occasionally gathering at the base of gnarled trees upon whose palsied arms leaves hung as an apparent afterthought. In the field beyond, high grass flowed beneath the gentle caress of the slightest of breezes. The land was framed by dying walnut trees, rotten arms severed by lightning long gone, poking up into the sky as if vying for the attention of a deity who could save them. A killdeer fluttered its wings in feigned distress and hopped across the gravel path in front of the two boys, hoping to lead them away from a nest it had concealed somewhere nearby.

"Think we should follow it?" Timmy asked in a tone that suggested he found the idea about as interesting as trying to run up a tree.

"All I can think of is the pond," Pete muttered. "We could go fishing."

"My pole's broken. So's yours, remember?"

Pete nodded. "Oh yeah. The swordfight."

"That *I* won."

"No you didn't."

"I sure did. I snapped yours first."

"No way," said Pete, more alive than Timmy had seen him in days. "They both snapped at the same time!"

"Whatever."

"'Whatever' yourself."

They walked in silence for a moment, the brief surge of animosity already fading in the heat. A hornet buzzed Pete's ear and he yelped as he flapped a hand at it. Timmy laughed and once the threat had passed, Pete did too. The echoes of their mirth hung in the muggy air.

They came to a bend in the path where the ground was softer and rarely dry even in summer. The passage of the construction crew had made ridges in the earth here, an obstacle the boys tackled with relish. This in turn led to a crude wooden bridge which consisted of two planks nailed together and flung haphazardly across an overgrown gully. Beneath the bridge, a thin stream of dirty water trickled sluggishly over the rocks and cracked concrete blocks the builders had tossed in to lighten their load.

Myers Pond—named after the doctor and his sons who'd built it one summer long before Timmy was born—had managed to remain unspoiled and unpolluted thus far. It was a welcome sight as the boys fought their way through grass that had grown tall in their absence.

The boy already sitting there, however, wasn't.

Pete paused and scratched furiously at his shoulder, waiting for Timmy to say what they were both thinking. They were standing where a wide swath of grass had been trampled flat, the slope of the bank mere feet away. A dragonfly hovered before the frail-looking boy on the bank as if curious to see what this new intruder had in mind, then zipped away over the shimmering surface of the pond.

Timmy looked at Pete and whispered: "Do you know that kid?"

Pete shook his head. "Do you?"

"No."

The pond was shared by many of the neighborhood kids, a virtual oasis in the summer if you were brave enough to stalk forth amongst the legion of ticks and chiggers, but few people swam there. The story went that when Doctor Myers built the pond all those years ago, he'd filled it with baby turtles, and that now those babies had grown to the size of Buicks, hiding down where the water was darkest, waiting for unsuspecting toes to come wiggling.

Had it been another boy from the neighborhood, Timmy wouldn't have cared. But this wasn't any kid he had ever seen before, and while it was common for other children to visit their friends around here, they seldom came this far from the safety of the houses.

And this kid was odd looking, even odder looking than Pete.

He sat so close to the water they could almost hear gravity groaning from the strain of keeping him from falling in. He didn't wear shorts as the burgeoning heat demanded but rather a pair of long gray trousers with a crease in the middle, rolled up so that a bony ankle showed, the rest of his foot submerged in the slimy green fringe of the water, bobbing up and down like a lure.

His impossibly large hands—*adult hands*, Timmy thought—were splayed out behind him, whiter still than the chalky foot and even from where Timmy stood, he could see those fingers were tipped with black crescents of dirt.

He nudged Pete, who jumped as if bitten.

"*What?*"

"Go talk to him," Timmy said, a half-smile on his face, knowing his friend would balk at the idea. Pete raised copper eyebrows and scoffed as quietly as he could.

Not quietly enough, however. For the kid turned and spotted them, his eyes like bullets gleaming in the sunlight as he appraised them. His hair was shorn away in patches, contrasting with the long greasy brown clumps that sank beneath and sprouted from the collar of his ripped black T-shirt. The exposed patches of scalp were an angry red.

"Who are you?" Timmy asked, stumbling out of his amazement and horror at the appearance of the stranger and composing himself, ready at a moment's notice to look tough.

The chalk foot bobbed. All three boys watched it and then the kid smiled at them. Pete backed up a step, a low groan coming from his throat like a trapped fly, and Timmy found he had to strain to avoid doing something similar. If someone had whispered an insult to his mother into his ear, he wouldn't have been any less disturbed than he was by that smile. It was crooked, and wrong. Something pricked his ankle. He looked down and hissing, slapped away a mosquito. When he straightened, the boy was standing in front of him and this time he couldn't restrain a yelp of surprise.

Up close the kid looked even more peculiar, as if his face were the result of a shortsighted child's mix-n'-match game. His eyes were cold dark stones, set way too far apart, and reminded Timmy of the one and only catfish he had ever caught in this pond. He wondered if there was something wrong with the kid; maybe he'd gone crazy after being bitten by a rabid squirrel or something. Stuff like that happened, he knew. He'd heard the stories.

The kid's head looked like a rotten squash beaten and decorated to resemble a human being's and his mouth could have been a recently healed wound…or a burn.

Instinct told him to run and only the steady panting behind him told him that Pete hadn't already fled. A soft breeze cooled the sweat on the nape of his neck, and he swallowed, flinched when a bug's legs tickled his cheek.

The kid's eyes were on him and Timmy couldn't keep from squirming. It was as if his mother had caught him looking at a girl's panties. His cheeks burned with shame.

And then the kid spoke: "Darryl," he said in words spun from filaments of phlegm, making it sound as if he needed to clear his throat.

It took Timmy a moment to decipher what he'd heard and to realize it wasn't a threat, or an insult, or a challenge. The last thing he had expected from the creepy-looking boy was a simple answer. He felt his shoulders drop a notch.

"Oh. Hi. I'm...uh...Timmy." The moment the words crawled from his mouth, he regretted them. Without knowing why, he felt more in danger now that he'd revealed his name.

The boy stared back at him and nodded. "This your pond?" he asked, cocking his strangely shaped head towards the water.

Timmy's mind raced, quickly churning possible responses into something coherent. What emerged was: "Yes. No." *Aw crap.*

The boy said nothing but grinned a grin of ripped stitches and turned back to look out over the water. Pine and walnut trees clustered together on the far side of the pond and some distance beyond them lay the train tracks. Timmy found himself wondering if the kid had been traveling the trains and jumped off to see what trouble he could cause in Delaware. He sincerely hoped not and was suddenly very conscious of how far away from the houses they were. Would anyone hear a scream?

A sudden gust of wind hissed high in the trees and a twisted branch overhanging the pond dipped its leaves into the water as if checking the temperature.

The kid slid back down to his spot on the bank and returned his foot to the drifting pond scum. Out in the water, a red and white bobber rode the miniature waves: memento of a past fisherman's unsuccessful cast.

"What are you doing, anyway?" Timmy asked without knowing he was going to. He made a silent promise to himself never to argue again when his father told him he asked too many questions.

The boy answered without raising his head. "Feeding the turtles."

The gasp from behind him made Timmy spin in Pete's direction. Pete had a hand clamped over his mouth, his face even paler than usual, his freckles gray periods on an otherwise blank page. He pointed at the boy and Timmy looked back, expecting to see the kid had jumped to his feet again and was brandishing a knife or something worse. But Darryl hadn't moved, except for his foot, which he continued to let rise and fall into the cool water. Except this time,

Timmy watched it long enough, watched it come back up out of the water and saw that a ragged semicircle of the boy's ankle was missing, the skin around it mottled and sore. Blood plinked into the water as the boy lowered it again and smiled that ugly smile to himself.

Pete's urgent whisper snapped Timmy out of the terrible and fascinating sight of what Darryl had called 'feeding the turtles.'

"Timmy, *c'mon*. Let's get *out* of here. There's something *wrong* with that kid." He emphasized every couple of words with a stamp of his foot and Timmy knew his friend was close to tears. In truth, he wasn't far away from weeping himself. But not here. Not in front of the crazy kid. Who knew what that might set off in him?

He stepped back, unable to take his eyes off the boy and his ravaged ankle, rising and falling like a white seesaw over the water.

"We're going now," he said, unsure why he felt the need to announce their departure when the element of surprise might have suited them better.

The boy dipped his foot and this time Timmy could have sworn he saw something small, dark and leathery rising to meet it. He moved back until he collided with Pete, who grabbed his wrist hard enough to hurt.

As Timmy was about to turn, Darryl's head swiveled toward him, the frostiness of his gaze undeniable now. "See you soon," he said. Timmy felt gooseflesh ripple across his skin.

They didn't wait to see what might or might not be waiting with open mouths beneath the boy's ankle. Instead, they turned and made their way with a quiet calm that begged to become panic, through the weeds and the tall grass until they were sure they could not be seen from the pond. And then they ran, neither of them screaming in terror for fear of ridicule later when this all turned out to be a cruel dream.

2

THAT NIGHT, AFTER SHOWERING and checking for the gamut of burrowers and parasites the pond had to offer, Timmy slipped beneath the cool sheets, more glad than he'd ever been before that his father was there to read to him.

Beside his bed, a new fan had been lodged in the open window and droned out cool air as his father yawned, set his Coke down on the floor between his feet and smiled. "You remember where we left off?" he asked as he took a seat just below his son's toes.

Timmy nodded. They were reading *The Magician's Nephew* by C.S. Lewis. He smoothed the blankets over his chest. "Queen Jadis turned out to be really wicked. She wanted to go with Digory and Polly back to their world to try to take it over, but they touched the rings and escaped."

His father nodded. "Right." As he flipped through the pages, Timmy looked around the room, his eyes settling on the fish his father had painted on the walls last summer. They were tropical fish; brightly colored and smudged where the paint had tried to run. A hammerhead shark had been frozen in the act of dive-bombing the wainscoting. Here a hermit crab peeked out from the shadows of his sanctuary; there a jellyfish mimicked the currents to rise from the depths of the blue wall. A lobster waved atop a rock strategically placed to hide a crack in the plaster. Bubbles rose toward the ceiling and Timmy tracked them with fearful eyes down to the half open mouth of a gaudily painted turtle.

He listened to his father read, more comforted by the soft tone and occasional forced drama of his voice than the words themselves.

When his father reached a page with a picture, he turned the book around to show it to Timmy. It was a crosshatching of the fearsome queen, one arm curled behind her head, the other outstretched before a massive black metal door as she readied herself to fling it wide with her magic. Timmy nodded, indicating he'd seen enough, and his father went back to reading.

Timmy's eyes returned to the crudely drawn turtle on the wall. It was bigger than any turtle he'd ever seen, and the mouth was a thin black line twisted slightly at the end to make it appear as if it was smiling—his father's touch. The shell was enormous, segmented into hexagonal shapes and much more swollen than he imagined they were in real life. Was it something like this, then, that had been chewing on Darryl's ankle? The thought brought a shudder of revulsion rippling through him and he pulled the sheets closer to his chin. It couldn't have been. Even a kid as crazy-looking as Darryl couldn't have done such a thing without it hurting him. Perhaps the boy had been injured and was merely soaking his wound in the pond when they found him. Perhaps it had all been a trick, a bit of mischief they had fallen for, hook line and sinker. That made much more sense, and yet he still didn't believe it. The cold knot in his throat remained and when his father read to him of Digory's and Polly's escape from Charn and their arrival—with the queen in tow—at the mysterious pools in the Wood between the Worlds, he wondered if they had seen a boy there, sitting on the bank of one of those pools, his feet dipped in the water.

"Dad?"

His father's eyebrows rose above his thick spectacles. "What is it?"

Timmy looked at him for a long time, struggling to frame the words so they wouldn't sound foolish, but almost all of it sounded ridiculous. Eventually he sighed and said: "I was at the pond today."

"I know. Your mother told me. She tugged a few ticks off you too, I believe. Nasty little buggers, aren't they?"

Timmy nodded. "I saw someone down there." He cleared his throat. "A boy."

"Oh yeah? A friend of yours?"

"No. I've never seen this kid before. He was dirty and smelly, and his head was a funny shape. Weird eyes, too."

The eyebrows lowered. "'Weird' how?"

"I-I don't know. They had no color, just really dark."

"What was he doing down there?"

"Just sitting there," Timmy said softly, avoiding his father's eyes.

"Did he say anything to you?"

After a moment of careful thought, Timmy nodded. "He said he was feeding the turtles." There was silence then, except for the hum of the fan.

Timmy's father set the book down beside him on the bed and crossed his arms. "And was he?" he said at last, as if annoyed that Timmy hadn't already filled in that gap in the story.

"I don't know. There was a piece of his foot missing and he was—"

His father sighed and waved a hand. "Okay, okay. I get it. Ghost story time, huh?" He stood up and Timmy quickly scooted himself into a sitting position, his eyes wide with interest.

"You think he was a ghost?" he asked, as his father smirked down at him.

"Well isn't that how the story is supposed to go? Did you turn back when you were leaving only to find the boy had mysteriously vanished?"

Timmy slowly shook his head. "We didn't look back. We were afraid to."

His father's smile held but seemed glued there by doubt. "There's no such thing as ghosts, Timmy. Only *ghost* stories. The living have enough to worry about these days without the dead coming back to complicate things. Now you get some rest."

He carefully stepped around his Coke and leaned in to give Timmy a kiss on the cheek. Ordinarily, the acrid stench of his father's cologne bothered him, but tonight it was a familiar smell, a smell he knew was real, and unthreatening.

"Good night, Dad."

"Good night, kiddo. I'll see you in the morning." He walked, Coke in hand, to the door. "Have sweet dreams now, you hear me? Don't go wasting any more time and energy on ghosts and goblins. Nothing in the dark you can't see in the daylight. Remember that."

Timmy smiled weakly. "I will. Thanks."

His father nodded and closed the door, but just as the boy had resigned himself to solitude and all the fanciful and awful ponderings that would be birthed within it, the door opened again and his father poked his head in.

"One more thing."

"Yeah?"

"I don't want you going back to the pond for a while. You know, just in case there are some odd folk hanging around down there."

"Okay."

"Good boy. See you in the morning."

"See you in the morning too." His father started to close the door.

"Dad?"

A sigh. "Yes?"

"Do you think there are turtles back there? Like, big ones?"

"Who knows? I've never seen them but that isn't to say they aren't there. Now quit worrying about it and get some sleep."

"I will."

"Goodnight."

The door closed and Timmy listened to his father's slippers slopping against the bare wood steps of the stairs. It was followed by mumbled conversation and Timmy guessed his mother was being filled in on The Turtle Boy story. Her laughter, crisp and warm, echoed through the house.

Timmy turned his back on the aquatic renderings and stared at his *Hulk* poster on the opposite wall. As he replayed moments from his favorite episodes of the show, he found himself drifting, edging closer to the bank of sleep where he sat among ugly children with wounded feet and burst stitches for smiles.

3

THE NEXT MORNING, he went to Pete's house and found him in his sun-washed kitchen, hunched over a bowl of cereal as if afraid someone was going to steal it.

"Hi Pete."

Pete looked positively bleached. Except for the angry purple bruise around his left eye. "Hi."

"Ouch. Where did you get the shiner?"

"Fell."

"Where?"

Pete shrugged but said nothing further and while this wasn't unusual, Timmy sensed his friend was still shaken from their meeting with Darryl the day before. He, on the other hand, had managed to convince himself that they had simply stumbled upon some sick kid from one of the neighboring towns who had ventured out of his camp to see what the city had to offer. Pete's father had once told the boys about the less prosperous areas of Delaware and warned them not to ride their bikes there after sundown. He'd frightened them with stories about what had happened to those children who'd disobeyed their parents and ventured there after dark. They had resolved never to step foot outside their own neighborhood if they could help it. Of course, they couldn't stop people from coming *into* their neighborhood either, and after much musing, Timmy had decided that that was exactly what had happened. Nothing creepy going on, just a kid sniffing around in uncharted territory. No big deal. And though he'd been scared to stumble upon the strange kid with the mangled foot, the fear had buckled under the weight of solid reasoning and now he felt more than a little silly for panicking.

It appeared, however, that the waking nightmare had yet to let Pete go. The longer Timmy watched him, the more worried he became. It didn't help that Pete was accident-prone. Every other week he had some kind of injury to display.

"You all right, Pete?" he asked as he slid into a chair.

Pete nodded and made a snorting sound as he shoveled a spoonful of Cheerios into his mouth. A teardrop of milk ran from the corner of his mouth, dangled from his chin, then fell back into the white sea beneath his face. A smile curled

Timmy's lips as he recalled his mother saying: "If you ever eat like that kid, you'd better be prepared to hunt for your own food. Honestly, you'd think they starve him over there or something."

When Pete finished, he raised the bowl to his lips and drained the remaining milk from it, then wiped a forearm across his lips and belched softly.

"So, what should we do today?" Timmy asked, already bored with the stale atmosphere in Pete's house.

Pete shrugged but the reply came from the hallway behind them.

"He's not doing anything today. He's grounded."

Timmy turned in his chair. It was Pete's father.

Wayne Marshall was tall and thin; his skin brushed with the same healthy glow nature had denied his son. He wore silver wire-rimmed glasses atop an aquiline nose. Thick black eyebrows sat like a dark horizon between the sweeping black wings of his bangs. He was frightening when angry, but Timmy seldom stuck around to see the full force of his wrath. Right now, it seemed he was on 'simmer.'

"What were you two boys doing back at Myers Pond yesterday?" he asked as he strode into the kitchen and plucked an errant strand of hair from his tie. From what

Timmy had seen, the man only owned two suits—one black, the other a silvery gray. Today he wore the former, with a white shirt and a red and black striped tie.

He looked at Pete, but the boy was staring into his empty bowl as if summoning the ghost of his Cheerios.

Timmy swallowed. "We were looking for something to do. We thought we might go fishing but our poles are broken."

Mr. Marshall nodded. As he poured himself a coffee, Timmy noticed no steam rose from the liquid as it surged into the cup. *Cold coffee?* It made him wonder how early these people got up in the morning. After all, it was only eight-thirty now.

"The new Zebco pole I bought Petey for his birthday a few months back, you mean?"

Timmy grimaced. "I didn't know it was a new one. He never told me that."

The man leaned against the counter and studied Timmy with obvious distaste and the boy felt his face grow hot under the scrutiny. He decided Pete had earned himself a good punch for not rescuing him.

"Yeah well…." Pete's father said, pausing to sip from his cup. He smacked his lips. "There isn't much point going back to the pond if you're not going fishing, is there? I mean, what else is there to do?"

Timmy shrugged. "I dunno. Stuff."

"What kind of stuff?"

Another shrug. His mother had warned him about shrugging when asked a direct question, and how irritating it was to grown-ups, but at that moment he felt like his shoulders were tied to counterweights and threaded through eyehooks in the ceiling.

"Messin' around and stuff. You know...playing army. That kind of stuff."

"What's wrong with playing army out in the yard, or better still in *your* yard with all the trees you've got back there?"

"I don't know."

The urge to run infected him, but his mind kept a firm foot on the brakes. He had already let his yellow belly show once this week; it wasn't going to happen again now, no matter how cranky Mr. Marshall was feeling this morning. But it was getting progressively harder to return the man's gaze, and although he had seen Pete's dad lose his cool more than once, he wasn't sure he had ever felt this much animosity coming from him. The sudden dislike was almost palpable.

Mr. Marshall's demeanor changed. He sipped his coffee and grinned, but there was a distinct absence of humor in the expression. His smoldering glare shifted momentarily to Pete, who shuffled in response. Timmy felt his spine contract with discomfort.

"Petey was telling me about this Turtle Boy you boys are supposed to have met."

At that moment, had Timmy eyes in the back of his head, they would have been glaring at Pete. He didn't know why. After all, he had told his father. But *his* father hadn't blown a gasket over some busted fishing poles, Zebco or no Zebco, and had waved away the idea of a ghost at Myers Pond without a second thought.

The way Mr. Marshall was looking at him now, it appeared he had given it a *lot* of thought.

"Yeah. It was weird," he said with a lopsided grin.

"Weird? It scared Pete half to death and from what he tells me you were scared too. Didn't your mother ever tell you not to talk to strangers?"

"Yes, but it was just a ki—"

"Don't you know how many children disappear every year around this area? Most of them because they wandered off to places they were warned not to go. Places like that pond, and while I don't believe for a second that either of you saw anything like Pete described, I don't want you bringing my boy back there again, do you understand me?"

"But I didn't—"

"I spent most of last night prying ticks off him. Is that your idea of fun, Timmy?"

"No sir."

"I told him not to hang around with you anyway. You're trouble. Just like your father."

Caught in the spotlight cast by the morning sun, dust motes seemed to slow through air made thick with tension.

Timmy's jaw dropped. While he had squirmed beneath his friend's father's angry monologue, this insult to his own father made something snap shut in his chest. Anger and hurt swelled within him and he let out a long, infuriated breath. Unspoken words flared in that breath and died harmlessly before a mouth sealed tight with disgust. He felt his stomach begin to quiver and suddenly he wanted more than anything to be gone from Pete's house. The departure would come with the implied demand that Pete go to hell in a Zip-Loc bag, the sentiment punctuated by a slamming of the front door that would no doubt bring Mr. Marshall running to chastise him further.

Fine, he thought, the words poison arrows in his head. *Let him. He can go to hell in a baggie too.*

"I gotta go now," he mumbled finally, and without sparing his treacherous comrade a glance, started toward the front door.

Hot tears blurred the hallway and the daylight beyond as he left the house and closed the door *gently* behind him. The anger had ebbed away as quickly as it had come, replaced now by a tiny tear in the fabric of his happiness through which dark light shone. He was dimly aware of the door opening behind him.

Pete's voice halted him and he turned. "Hey, I'm sorry Timmy. Really I am."

"Oh yeah?" The hurt spun hateful words he couldn't speak. With what looked like monumental effort, Pete closed the front door behind him. With an uncertain smile, he said: "My Dad'll kill me for this, but let's go do something."

"Good idea," Timmy said, aware that an errant tear was trickling down his cheek. "You can go to hell. I'm going home."

"Timmy, wait I—"

"Shut up, Pete. I *hate* you!"

He ran home and slammed the door behind him. His mother sat wiping her eyes, engrossed in some soppy movie. He waited behind the sofa for her to ask him what was wrong and when she didn't, he ran to his room and to bed, where he lay with his face buried in the cool white pillows.

And seethed.

4

THAT NIGHT, HE DREAMT he was standing at his bedroom window.

Down in the yard, beside the pine tree, a boy stood wreathed in shadow, despite the cataract eye of the moon soaring high in the sky behind him.

And though the window was closed, Timmy heard him whisper: "Would you die for him?"

He squinted to see more than just shadow, his heart filled with dread.

"Darryl?"

And then he woke, warmed by the morning sun, nothing but the distant echo of the whisper in his mind.

5

S HORTLY AFTER MR. MARSHALL made his feelings known about Timmy and his father, he sent Pete to summer camp.

Although the anger and hurt had settled like a stone in the pit of his belly, Timmy missed Pete and hoped Mr. Marshall would realize his cruelty and allow things to return to normal before Timmy found himself minus a friend. Summer was only just beginning, and he didn't relish the idea of trudging through it without his best buddy.

Early the next Saturday, he came home from riding his bike to find his parents grinning at him in a way he wasn't sure he'd ever seen before. It made his heart lurch; he couldn't decide if it was a good or a bad thing.

"What?" he asked. They were sitting next to each other at the kitchen table, looking fresh and content. His mother was looping a strand of her hair around her finger, his father nodding slowly. They almost looked *proud*. As soon as

Timmy's eyes settled on the source of their amusement, he felt as if someone had forced his finger into a light socket.

Kim Barnes.

"What is she doing here?" he asked, pointing at the black-haired girl with the braces who stood in the hallway behind them. Her arms were crossed, and she shifted from foot to foot as if no happier about where she had found herself than he.

His mother scowled. "Is that any way to talk to a lady? Kim's sister and her friend have gone to camp too, so she has no one to play with for the whole summer. Isn't that a nice coincidence?"

Timmy was appalled. "She's a *girl!*"

"No flies on him," said his father.

"But...she doesn't even *like* me!"

"Now how do you know that? Have you ever asked her?"

"I know she doesn't. She's always making faces at me in school."

Kim smiled. "I don't mean anything by it."

"You see," his mother said. "You have to give a girl a chance."

Timmy felt sick.

"I don't have to play with you if you don't want me to," Kim said in a pitiful tone. Timmy felt an ounce of hope but knew his parents, who melted at the sound of her feigned sorrow, would vanquish it.

"Don't be silly. Timmy would love to play with you, wouldn't you, Timmy?"

He sighed and studied the scuffed toe of his sneakers. "I guess so."

"Speak up, son."

"I guess so," he repeated, wondering how this summer could possibly get any worse.

His mother went to Kim. With maternal grace, she eased the girl into the kitchen. Timmy felt the color rise in his cheeks and looked away.

"Now see," his mother said. "Why don't you both go on outside in the sunshine and see what you can find to do. I bet you'll get along just fine."

I bet we won't, Timmy thought, miserable. With a heavy sigh, he turned and opened the door.

6

THEY WERE STANDING IN THE YARD, Kim with her arms still folded and Timmy watching the bloated white clouds sailing overhead when she said: "I didn't want to come over here, you know."

Without looking at her he scoffed. "Then, why did you?"

"Your mom called my mom and told her you were bored and lonely and—"

"I wasn't *lonely*. I was doing just fine."

"Well, your mom thought you weren't and asked if I could come over. I told *my* mom I didn't want to play with you because you are dirty and smelly."

Timmy gaped at her. "Really?"

She shook her head and he had to restrain the sigh that swelled in his throat.

"So, I guess we'll have to do something for a while at least," she said. "What do you want to play?"

"Not dolls, anyway. I hate dolls." He watched a blue jay until it flew behind her. Tracking it any further would have meant looking in her direction and he wasn't yet ready to do that.

"Me too," Kim said, startling him, and he looked at her. Briefly.

"I thought *all* girls liked dolls."

He saw her shrug. "I think they're dumb."

"Real dumb."

"Yeah."

The silence wasn't as dreadful as Timmy had thought it would be. For one, she didn't like dolls and that was a plus. Dolls really were dumb. He hadn't said it just to annoy her. And at least she *talked*. By now he'd have grown tired of listening to himself talking to Pete and getting no answer. So, he guessed, she wasn't *that* bad.

But still, he didn't like the idea of being seen hanging around with her. No matter how cool she might turn out to be, if anyone at school heard about it, they'd say he was in love with her or something and that they were going to have a baby. And that would be bad news. *Real* bad news.

"Why don't we go back to the pond?" she asked then, as if reading his thoughts.

Going back to Myers Pond was no more comforting an idea than hanging around with a girl, but at least there no one would see them together.

"I'm not allowed to go back to the pond," he said, with an ounce of shame. Admitting you were restricted by the same rules as everyone else seemed akin to admitting weakness when you said it to a girl.

"Why not?"

"I'm just not."

When she said nothing, he gave a dramatic sigh and conceded. "Pete Marshall's dad thinks there might be some creeps back there or something. He thinks it might be dangerous for kids. My dad doesn't want me going back there either."

"Creeps? Like what kind of creeps?"

He almost told her but caught himself at the last minute and shrugged it off. "Just some strange kids."

She stared at him for a moment and he struggled not to cringe.

"Like the Turtle Boy?"

Now he looked at her and through the shock of hearing the name he had given Darryl, he realized she wasn't so ugly and stinky and everything else he associated with the chittering group she swept around the playground with at recess. Her eyes, for one thing, were like sparkling emeralds, and once he peered into them his discomfort evaporated, and he had to struggle to look away. Her skin reminded him of his mother's soap and that conjured a memory of a pleasant clean smell. But still…she was a girl and that made him feel a strange kind of awkwardness.

"What?" she said after a moment.

Eventually he composed himself enough to croak: "You've seen him?"

"Yes. He's awful creepy looking, isn't he?"

"But…when did *you* see him?"

"The first day of summer vacation. My cousin Dale came to visit with his mom, and we went fishing back there." She gave him a shy smile. "I'm not much good at fishing. I lost my bobber."

Timmy remembered the small red and white ball drifting in the water the day they'd seen Darryl and wondered if it was hers.

"Dale caught a catfish. It was ugly and gross and when he reeled it in, he raised it up in front of my face and tried to get me to kiss it. I ran into the trees and that's where he was. The Turtle Boy. He stank really bad and looked at me as if I had caught him doing something he shouldn'ta been. I was scared."

Timmy was confused. "But why do you call him that? Did he tell you that was his name?"

"No. I just...I don't know. I just remember thinking about it later and that's the name I gave him."

"That's weird. That's the name *I* gave him."

"I guess that is weird."

"Have you ever seen him around before?"

She shook her head. "Have you?"

"No, but I wish I knew why he was here and where he came from."

A blur of movement caught his eye and he followed it to a groundhog shimmying his way along the bottom of the yard toward the road. He looked back to Kim. "Did he say anything to you?"

"Yeah." She swallowed and the same fear that had gripped him when he'd seen Darryl's ankle was written across her face. It made him feel better somehow to see it. It meant he was no longer alone in his fear. With Pete it wasn't the same. Pete was afraid to ride his bike on the off chance he might fall and get hurt. He was also afraid of storms and dogs and pretty much anything that moved and had teeth.

"He said: 'They're hungry.'"

"When me and Pete saw him, he was putting his heel into the water. There was a piece of it missing. He said he was feeding the turtles. What do you suppose it means?"

"There's only one way to find out," she said.

"How?"

Kim's braces segmented her mischievous smile but couldn't take away the appeal of it. A slight smile crept across Timmy's lips in response. He got the feeling that even though The Turtle Boy had frightened her, she wasn't easily deterred from any kind of adventure.

"We have to ask him, of course."

7

RATHER THAN TAKING THE REGULAR gravel path back to the pond, a path that could be spotted from most of the houses, they cut across Mr. Patterson's field, pausing only to look at the large puddle, which was all that remained of the hole Timmy and Pete had been digging. A pile of earth like a scale-model mountain sat next to it.

"We were looking for gold," he explained.

"Did you find any?" Kim asked.

He shrugged, strangely ashamed. "No. We found some red clay though."

Kim smiled. "Maybe that would be worth something in some other country. Maybe some country where they have gold to spare and kids dig for red clay?"

He nodded, a silly grin breaking out across his face. He knew it was a foolish notion—he'd never heard of a place that had *too* much gold—but it was a nice fantasy, and he silently thanked her for not making fun of his efforts.

They carried on through the high grass, chasing crickets and wondering what kind of exotic creatures they heard scurrying at their approach. The field ran parallel to the gravel path, but the trees shielded them from view, and they hunkered down, the grass whipping against their bare legs. Much to his surprise, Kim kept the pace as he raced toward the narrow dirt road leading into the pond. At times she drew abreast of him and, more than once—though he would never admit it—she began to inch ahead of him, forcing him to push himself until he felt his chest start to ache.

At last they reached the makeshift bridge. Kim, her legs braced on the wobbling boards, leaned over to catch her breath. She looked down at the stream trickling beneath them. "They've ruined it, haven't they?"

It took him a moment to realize what she was referring to and then he told her that yes, they had ruined it. The construction crews dedicated to tearing up the land they'd once played in seemed equally driven to foul whatever they'd been prohibited to touch. Gullies became dumping grounds for material waste, streams became muddied and paths cracked beneath the groaning and shrieking metal of their monstrous machines. Timmy joined her in a moment of mournful pondering at the senselessness of it all, then tapped her on the elbow and pointed up at the sky.

Shadows rushed past them, crawling through the grass toward the train tracks and spilling from the trees as the breeze gained strength. Over their heads, the sky had turned from blue to gray, the sun now a dim torch glimpsed through a caul of spider webs. All around them the trees began to sway and hiss as if the breeze were water, the canopies fire.

Kim nodded at the change and hurried to his side. She mumbled something to him, and he looked at her. "What?"

"I said: my dad says they're going to fill in the pond."

Before Timmy had met Darryl, this might have hurt him more than it did now. Still, it didn't seem right. "Why?"

"I don't know. He says in a few years all of this will be houses and that the pond is only in the way. Apparently, Doctor Myers's son sold this area of the land so they're just waiting for someone to buy it before they fill it in."

Timmy knew her father worked on a construction site across town and would no doubt be privy to such information. It was a depressing thought; not so much that they would be taking the pond away, but because he suspected that would only be the start of it. Soon, the fields would be gone, concrete lots in their place.

They carried on up the rise until the black mirror of the pond revealed itself. Timmy's gaze immediately went to the spot where he had seen Darryl, but he saw no one sitting there today. Kim walked on and over the bank and made her way around the pond toward the brace of fir trees weaving in the wind. She paused and looked back at him over her shoulder. "Are you coming?"

"Yeah."

But he was already starting to question the logic behind such a move. At least the last time he'd been here he'd had the escape route at his back; if The Turtle Boy had tried anything it wouldn't have been hard to turn and run. Going into those trees was like walking into a cage. You would have to thread your way through brambles and thick undergrowth to be clear of it. And even then, there was nowhere to run but the train tracks.

A quiver of fear rippled through him, and he masked it by smacking an imaginary mosquito from his neck. Overhead, the clouds thickened. With a sigh, he followed Kim into the trees.

On this side of the pond, dispirited pines hung low. The earth beneath was a tangle of withered needles, flattened grass, and severed branches. The children had to duck until they'd cleared the biggest and densest stand of pines.

At last they emerged on the other side, a marshy stretch of land that offered a clear view of the train tracks but soaked their sandaled feet.

After a moment of listening to the breeze and searching the growing shadows around them, Kim put her hands on her hips and looked at Timmy, who was preoccupied with trying to remove sticky skeins of spider web from his face.

"He's not here," she said, stifling a giggle at Timmy's dismay.

He didn't answer until he was sure some fat black arachnid hadn't nested in his hair. When he'd cleared the remaining strands, he grimaced and looked around. "Sure looks like it. Unless he's hiding."

"Maybe he's gone."

"Yeah, maybe." It was a comforting thought. Behind them in the distance, the hungry heavens rumbled as God made a dark stew of the sky. "Maybe he caught a train out of here."

Kim glanced toward the tracks, which were silent and somehow lonely without a thousand pounds of steel shrieking over them. "Or maybe a train caught *him*."

Before Timmy could allow the image to form in his mind, he heard something behind him, on the other side of the pines.

"Did you hear that?"

Kim shook her head.

A twig snapped and they both backed away.

"It's probably a squirrel or something," Kim whispered, and Timmy was suddenly aware that her hand was gripping his. He looked down at it, then at her, but she was intent on the movement through the trees behind them. He ignored the odd but not entirely unpleasant sensation of her cool skin on his and held his breath. Listening.

"Maybe a deer," Kim said, so low Timmy could hardly hear her above the breeze.

They stood like that for what seemed forever, ears straining to filter the sounds from the coiling weather around them. Timmy could hear little over the thundering of his own heart. Kim was holding his hand even tighter now. A terrifying thought sparked in his mind: *Does this mean she's my girlfriend?*

"C'mon," he said at last. "There's no one there."

She nodded and they both stepped forward.

Timmy was filled with confused excitement. Then, just as quickly, uncertainty came over him. Was she waiting for *him* to let go of *her* hand? Was she feeling uncomfortable and embarrassed now because he was holding her hand just as tightly? He tried to loosen his fingers, but she squeezed them, and a gentle wave of reassurance flooded over him.

She wasn't uncomfortable. She didn't want to let go. His heart began to race again but this time for a completely different reason.

And she continued to hold his hand. Continued even when something lithe and dark burst through the pines in front of their faces and dragged them both screaming through the trees.

8

TIMMY'S MOTHER OPENED THE FRONT DOOR. Her look of surprise doubled when she saw the rage on Wayne Marshall's face.

She stood in the doorway, leaning against the jamb. "What on earth is going on?" she said, crossing her arms. The gesture meant to convey that she was prepared to dispense blame wherever it was due.

On the porch, Pete's father still had a firm grip on the collar of Timmy's T-shirt, but he held Kim by the hand. Timmy felt strangely jealous.

"Sandra, I found these two snooping around back at Myers Pond," Mr. Marshall said firmly, as if this should be reason enough for punishment. Timmy's mother stared at him for a moment as if she didn't think so. Her gaze shifted briefly to Kim, then settled on her son.

"Didn't your father tell you not to go back there?"

Timmy nodded.

"Then, why did you? And I suppose you dragged poor Kimmie back with you, back into all that mud and sludge? Look at your sandals. I only bought them last week and you've wrecked them already." She shook her head and sighed. After a moment in which no one said anything, she looked at Mr. Marshall. "You can let them go now, Wayne. I don't think they're going to run away."

But he didn't release them, and Timmy thought he could feel the man's arms trembling with anger. In a voice little better than a growl, he said, "Sandra, it's not safe for kids back there. I don't think I have to remind you what happened a few years ago. I know I certainly don't want Pete back there and it's becoming blindingly obvious that your son has taken the role of the neighborhood Piper, leading everyone else's kids back there to get into all sorts of trouble."

A hard look entered Mrs. Quinn's eyes. "Now wait just a second—"

"If you had any sense, you'd send this little pup away for the summer like I sent Pete. It's the only way to keep them out of trouble. I mean, what was your son doing back there on the other side of the trees? With a *girl?* Is this the kind of thing you're letting him do behind your back?"

Timmy's mother straightened, her eyes blazing. "Just what the hell are you saying, Wayne? That because we don't shelter our boy and scream and roar commands at him around the clock that we're doing a bad job? Is that what you're saying? How about you mind your own business and let me raise my child how I see fit? Or would that be asking too much of you? He's eleven years old for God's sake, not a teenager."

"Just what I expected," Mr. Marshall said with a humorless smile. "All the time strolling around like you're Queen of the Neighborhood, better than everyone else. Well, I'm afraid your superior attitude seems to be lost on your kid."

"That's rich coming from you. At least Timmy doesn't live in fear of me."

"Maybe he damn well *should* live in fear of you."

"Watch your language in front of the children."

"*Fuck* the children!" He wrenched Timmy's collar hard enough to make the boy gasp. "You don't keep a watch on them. You don't care what happens to them. You let them wander and that's how they get hurt. It's bitches like you that make the world the way it is."

The trembling in his arms intensified, spreading through Timmy and making him queasy. He tried to pull away, but the man held firm. When he looked up, he saw that Mr. Marshall's face was swollen with rage.

"Let them go."

He didn't.

Timmy's mother took a step forward, teeth clenched. "I *said*, let them go, Wayne. Let them go and get the hell off my property or we're going to have a serious problem."

Mr. Marshall dropped Kim's wrist. Timmy felt the grip on his T-shirt loosen. They went to his mother's side. Mrs. Quinn tousled their hair and told them to go into the kitchen. As they did, Timmy heard Mr. Marshall mutter darkly, "We already have a problem."

9

AFTER MR. MARSHALL STORMED OFF, Timmy's mother made the kids some lemonade and ushered them into the living room. Timmy noticed the ice clinked more than usual as she set the glasses down on coasters for them, her smile flickering as much as the lights. She switched on the television and changed the channel to cartoons. *Spiderman* twitched and swung through the staticky skies of the city. Rain drummed impatient fingers on the roof. Kim scooted closer to Timmy and, though pleased, the boy guessed the image of Mr. Marshall's hands bursting from the trees was still lingering in her mind. Those hands had terrified him too. Even when he realized it was his friend's father that he was looking at and not the mangled squash countenance of The Turtle Boy, he hadn't felt much better. Or safer. Though Pete's dad had never been the friendliest of people, it seemed he'd become a monster since the start of summer.

They watched cartoons for a few hours until Timmy's father came home, cheerful though soaked from the hissing downpour. With a degree of shame, Timmy watched his father's good mood evaporate as his mother related the day's events. Kim shrank down further in her seat.

Eventually his father sat at the kitchen table with a fresh cup of coffee and called him over. His mother ferried a basket of laundry into the den and Kim watched with fretful eyes as he swallowed and slowly obeyed.

"Your mother tells me you were down at the pond today?"

"Yes, sir."

"Look at me when I'm talking to you."

Timmy felt as if his chin were the heaviest thing in the world. It was a titanic struggle to meet his father's eyes.

"Didn't we discuss this? Didn't I ask you to stay away from there?"

Timmy nodded.

"But you went anyway."

Timmy nodded again, his gaze drawn to his shoes until he caught himself and looked up.

His father stared for a moment and then shook his head as if he'd given up on trying to figure out some complicated math problem. "Why?"

"We were trying to find the Turtle Boy."

He expected his father to explode into anger, but to his surprise he simply frowned. "This is the kid you said you and Pete saw?"

"Yes, sir."

"Then you really did see a kid down there?"

"Yes, sir."

"Was everything you told me about him true, even the stuff about the wound he had?"

"It was horrible. He kept dipping it in the water. Said he was feeding the turtles."

His father nodded and poked his glasses back into the red indentation on the bridge of his nose. "It sounds like one of your comic book stories, but I believe you."

Timmy was stunned. "You do?"

"Yes. And I think the reason Mr. Marshall is so mad is because he's been drinking like a fish the past few weeks. It doesn't help to have you hanging around with his kid and making trouble."

"But I wasn't making tr—"

"I know, but the way he sees it you are. Wayne is going through a tough time, Timmy. His wife died, he started messing with…well, with bad stuff I don't really want to go into. He drinks too much and it's starting to get to him, to make him crazy, so I think it would be better to avoid him from now on."

This had never occurred to Timmy. His mind buzzed with possibilities. "But what about Pete?"

A sigh. "Son, I think it's time for you to start making new friends, like Kimmie there. Now, wait before you get upset. If you wanted to play with Pete, I wouldn't raise a hand to stop you, but I found out that Wayne put his house up for sale this morning. And with the way things are developing around here, he'll have it sold in a heartbeat, especially at the low price he's asking for it. So I don't think they're going to be our neighbors for much longer."

Timmy was appalled. "It's not fair. Pete's my best friend."

"I know," said his father, clamping a hand on Timmy's shoulder. "And God knows he's not having an easy time of it either. It's not right what Wayne's putting him through."

"What do you mean?"

"Never mind. I'm going to ask you now to stay away from Pete's dad, and this time I want you to promise you'll do as I say."

Timmy was buoyed a little by this new alliance in the dark world his summer had become. "I promise. He scares me anyway."

"Yes, I'm sure he does. He had no right to speak to you or your mother like he did. I'm going to go over there and have a few words with him."

Timmy felt something cold stir inside him, an icy current in the tide of pride he felt at his father's bravery.

"Don't."

His father nodded his understanding. "He's a bully, but only with kids. He'll think twice before crossing me, I guarantee it. He owes all of us an apology and I'll be damned if I'll let him be until I get it."

"Are you going to fight?"

"No. That's the last thing we'll do. You know how I feel about violence, what I tell *you* about violence."

"But...can't you go over there tomorrow?" Timmy gestured toward the rain-blurred kitchen window where the storm tugged at the fir trees. "It's nasty out there. You'll get drenched."

"Don't worry about it. I'm not exactly bone dry as it is."

"But—"

"Timmy, I won't be long. We'll just have a little chat, that's all."

But Timmy wasn't reassured. The storm was worsening, buffeting the house and blinding the windows. Lightning flashed, ravenous thunder at its heels, the sibilance of the rain an enraged serpent struggling to find entry through the cracks beneath the doors. It was the kind of weather when bad things happened, Timmy thought, the kind when monsters stepped out of the shadows to bask in the fluorescent light of the storm, drinking the rain and snatching those foolish enough to venture into their domain.

And his father wanted to do that very thing.

"Why don't you wait until the storm passes?" he asked, though he could see the resolve that had hardened his father's face when he shook his head and downed the dregs of his coffee.

"Timmy, there's nothing to worry about."

Timmy didn't agree. There was plenty to worry about, and as he watched his father stand and steel himself against the weather and the things it hid, he felt his legs weaken. A voice, calling feebly to him from the far side of the sweeping desert of his imagination, told him that he would remember this moment later, that summoning it would bring a taste of grief and regret and guilt. And failure. It would etch itself on his brain like an epitaph, inescapable and persistent, haunting his dreams. He felt he now stood at the epicenter of higher forces that revolved around him in the guise of a storm, that this little family play was taking place in its eye, tragedy waiting in the wings.

"I want to go with you."

Shrugging on his jacket, his father shook his head. "It'll only agitate him further."

"But you said he should apologize to me too, remember? You can ask him to apologize to me if I'm with you and I'd feel safer with you there."

His father studied him for a moment, then a small smile creased his lips as he dropped to his haunches and drew Timmy close. He hugged him hard and the boy felt a comforting warmth radiating from his father, mingled with the smell of aftershave.

"Timmy," he said softly, "I love you. You have no idea how hurt I am by what Wayne said to you. If I had been there, I'd probably have punched his lights out, so I'm glad I wasn't. Nobody has any right to speak to you like that and I don't want you to ever take any of it to heart. Wayne Marshall is a sick man, and a coward. Remember that. Your Mom and

I love you more than anything in this world and we're proud of you. That's all you need to know."

He rose to his feet. The movement seemed blurry and strange through the tears in Timmy's eyes. "*Please*," Timmy whispered, but his father was already walking toward the door.

10

AN HOUR PASSED.
Timmy sat in front of the television with Kim silent by his side.

His father had still not come home, and the worry made him sick to his stomach. His inner voice chastised him for letting his father go alone, but he quelled it with forced reassurance.

And then the power went out, darkness thick and suffocating descending around them. Kim gasped and grabbed his arm hard enough to hurt. He winced but did not ask her to release him. He welcomed the contact.

His mother arrived downstairs following a candle she had cupped with one slender hand. The yellow light made her face seem younger, less haunted, and the smile she wore was as radiant as the flame she set on the coffee table before them.

"Don't touch that or you'll burn yourself, if not the whole house," she told them. "I'll set up some more candles so we can see what we're doing. I don't like the idea of losing you in the dark."

Although she said it with humor, the phrase stuck with Timmy. *Losing you in the dark.* Was that what had happened to his father? Had he been lost in the dark? He was now more afraid than he could ever remember. Even more afraid than when he'd seen The Turtle Boy. He struggled to keep from trembling, something he was determined not to let happen. At least not while Kim was touching him.

"When's Dad coming home?" he asked, and saw his mother stiffen.

"Soon," she replied. "He's probably managed to calm Mr. Marshall down and they're discussing things man to man." She didn't sound like she believed it. "Wayne probably broke out the beers and the two of them are sitting out the storm and having a fine time." She laughed then, a sound forced and devoid of hope. Timmy shivered.

"Why don't you call and make sure?" he asked.

She sighed. "All right."

He watched her, dread stuck like a bone in his throat as she picked up the phone and stared for a moment at the shadows parrying with the light. After a few moments, she clucked her tongue and hung up.

"The phone's out," she told him.

Thunder blasted against the walls, making them all jump, and Kim let out a little squeal of fright.

Mom sighed and set about placing pools of amber light around the kitchen. They made twitching shadows and nervous silhouettes of the furniture.

"I hope he's okay," Timmy mumbled and Kim scooted closer. She was now close enough for him to feel her breath on his face. It was not an unpleasant feeling.

"He'll be fine," she said. "He's a big tough guy. Much bigger than Mr. Marshall. I bet if they got into a fight, your dad would knock him out in a second."

Timmy grinned. "You think so?"

"Sure!"

"Yeah, you're right. I bet he'd even knock some of his teeth out."

"Probably all of them. He wouldn't be so scary without those big white choppers of his."

They both laughed and, as if the sound had drawn her, his mother appeared beside them and perched herself on the arm of the sofa. "You two going to be all right?"

They nodded.

"Good. I think I'm going to go see what's keeping your father. Kim, if you want to come with me, I'll walk you home. It's not too far and you can borrow an umbrella if you like. I'm sure your mother is worried about you."

Timmy's throat constricted, his skin feeling raw and cold at the idea of being left alone while his mother and Kim ventured into Mr. Marshall's house.

What would he do if they left him and never came back? What would he do if they left him alone and Mr. Marshall came looking for him? What if he lost them *all* in the dark?

"Okay, Mrs. Quinn," said Kim. She sounded as if leaving was the last thing she wanted to do. She stood and Timmy opened his mouth to speak but nothing emerged.

"Guess I'll see you tomorrow?" she said, with a look he couldn't read in the candlelight.

He tried to make out her eyes, but the gloom had filled them with shadows.

"I'll go with you," he blurted, scrambling to his feet. He looked at his mother. "Mom, can I go too? I don't want to be by myself." He felt no shame at admitting this in front of Kim.

"No, Timmy. I want you to stay here. We won't be long."

"That's what Dad said, and he *has* been gone long!" Timmy said. "Please, let me go with you. This house gives me the creeps. I don't want to be here alone while you and Dad are over there with Mr. Marshall. He scares me."

Again, his mother sighed but he was already encouraged by the resignation in her expression. "Go on then, get your coat."

He raced to the mudroom and returned with a light blue windbreaker.

"You may need something heavier than that," his mother pointed out. "What happened to your gray one?"

"Ripped."

Timmy started moving toward the door. He waited while his mother cocooned Kim in one of her overcoats. She emerged looking chagrinned, lost inside the folds of a coat far too big for her. Timmy suppressed a laugh and then his mother handed them each an umbrella. They clustered by the sliding glass door, looking out at a blackness broken only by small rectangles of yellow light, and listened to the crackling roar of a storm not yet matured.

"How come the neighbors have got power and we don't?" Timmy asked.

"It happens that way sometimes. The lightning must have hit the transformer box on the side of our house. Let's go. Stay close to me," his mother said, and tugged the door aside.

They filed into the raging night, huddling against the needle spray of the rain. The wind thudded into them with insistent hands, attempting to drive them back; the air was filled with the scent of smoke and saturated earth. With the door closed and locked behind them, they bowed their heads and walked side by side to Wayne Marshall's house.

11

DESPITE THEIR FEARS—and Timmy was in no doubt now that they all shared the same ones—Mr. Marshall's porch was a welcome oasis from the storm. Timmy shuddered at the cold drops that trickled down his neck. Kim shivered, her hair hanging in sodden clumps like leaking shadows over the moon of her face. They snapped their umbrellas closed and his mother trotted up the three short steps to the front door.

It was already open.

His mother turned back to them, her face gaunt as she hurried them down from the porch and back into the rain.

"What is it?" Timmy asked, shouting to be heard above the shrieking wind. Sheets of icy rain lashed his face. Kim gave him a frightened look he figured probably mirrored his own. All he had seen as the door swung open had been a dark hall, broken at the end by the fluorescent glare from the kitchen. He was sure no one had been sitting at the table.

"Nothing," his mother called back. "Nothing at all. But I don't think they're here!"

Timmy felt as if his head had been dunked in ice water. His teeth clicked and an involuntary shiver coursed through him. Over their heads, a plastic lighthouse struggled valiantly to keep its wind chimes from tearing loose. The resultant muddle of jingles unsettled him. Mr. Marshall's weathervane groaned as it swung wildly from south to north and back again, adding to the discordant harmony of the turbulent night.

"Then, where are they?" Kim shouted, her arms crossed and buried beneath the coat as she danced from foot to foot.

But Timmy knew the answer.

"The pond," he said. His mother turned toward him and put a hand to her ear.

"The pond," he repeated. Another chill capered down his spine, like a flow of icy water.

"That's absurd," she said. "Why would they go back there? Especially on a night like this!"

Timmy shook his head, but in the wind, he heard his father: *I think the reason Mr. Marshall is so mad is because he's seen it too.*

It occurred to him then that The Turtle Boy—Darryl, or whoever he was—had come to Myers Pond not for Timmy, or Pete, or any of them. He had come for Mr. Marshall. And Mr. Marshall had been acting so strange, so angry because The Turtle Boy was tormenting him, *frightening* him.

But why?

It didn't make sense and the more he pondered it, the less likely it seemed. All he was sure of in that moment, standing in the pouring rain outside Mr. Marshall's house with the nervous white faces of his mother and Kim fixed on him, was that for whatever the reason, the men had gone to Myers Pond.

"I'm going to call the police," his mother said, already mounting the steps. "You two wait here and yell if you see them coming."

With that, she disappeared into the house, the door easing closed behind her.

Timmy turned.

"Hey!" Kim called and he looked back at her. She was a huddled mass of shadows, only a trembling lower lip visible through her hair. "Where are you going?"

"To the pond. I think Mr. Marshall is going to try to hurt my father. If we wait for the police, it might be too late."

"But what are you going to do? You're just a kid! You can't stop a grown-up if he wants to do something bad. Especially a *crazy* grown-up!"

Timmy shook his head. If Mr. Marshall intended to hurt his father, he at least had to *try* to stop it. He'd likely end up getting hurt in the process, but that didn't matter. He remembered his father reading to him, hugging him in the kitchen and telling him he loved him. He remembered riding his father's shoulders through the cornfields and feeling like the king of the world atop a throne. He remembered the disappointment of being in his first school play without his father present, only to see him creep to a seat next to his mother halfway through. He remembered the nightmares, the dreams in which he lost his father. He remembered the fear, the horror at being left alone without his father to live with the ghost of his mother.

No.

He would try. It was all he could do and just maybe it would make a difference. Determined, he stalked through the curtains of rain, flinching when the sky cracked above his head. He squinted through the temporary moonlight of the lightning, the mud sucking against the soles of his shoes.

"Timmy, wait!" Kim cried and he faltered at the far side of the house.

After a moment, he called to her: "Just tell my Mom where I'm going and not to worry."

"You idiot, of course she'll worry!"

"Just tell her!"

"Tell her yourself," Kim shouted, the hurt in her voice ringing over the raging wind.

He walked on until the ground hardened and stones rolled beneath his shoes. In a flash of lightning that sent stars waltzing across his field of vision, he saw the gravel winding ahead of him, emerging like a pale tongue from the black mouth of the weaving trees. Then the shade of night dropped once more and he was blinded, walking on a path from memory.

12

D AYLIGHT. Impossible and warm.

Mind numbing in its reality but most certainly there.

Eyes wide, Timmy stumbled and almost fell from the rain-swept night into a summer day.

This can't be happening. This isn't real.

But as he felt the sun start to warm his face, he knew it was real. The grass was dry against his ankles, the sky above the pond a stark, heavenly blue that bore no hint of rain. It was as if he'd stepped from real life onto a movie set, onto an authentic reproduction of Myers Pond on a summer day.

Timmy moved slowly, as if in a dream. Frogs croaked and toads belched in the reeds while dragonflies whirred over the unbroken surface of the water. Birds chirped and whistled, trilled and cawed and rustled in the trees. He glimpsed the rump of a deer, cotton-white tail twitching as it wandered away from the pond.

With his neck already aching from trying to take in all this magic at once, Timmy looked down to the bank where he had seen The Turtle Boy on that first day in another world. And there he was.

Darryl.

But not the scabrous, grotesque creature he and Pete had seen. No, this boy was smiling, fresh-faced and healthy, his skin pale but unmarked, devoid of weeping wounds and bites. His hair was parted neatly and shone in the midday sun, his gray trousers unsullied, the crease down the middle crisp and unruffled. His black t-shirt looked worn but not old. He did not seem to notice he was no longer alone, so intent was he in dipping his ankle into the cool water. Timmy watched as that ankle rose, expecting to see a glistening red wound, but the skin remained unbroken, unblemished. Pure. This, Timmy realized, was who The Turtle Boy had been before he'd changed into the malevolent, seething figure of decay and disease they'd found on the bank that day. This was Darryl before whatever had corrupted him had compelled him to feed himself to the turtles.

"Who are you?" Timmy asked softly but received no reply. Darryl continued to smile his knowing smile, continued to dip his smooth ankle into the calm waters.

"Why are you here?" Timmy demanded. For the first time, he noticed the small red notebook sitting next to the boy. He was almost tempted to reach down and grab the book, to read it, to search for the answers he could not get from the boy on the bank. But he didn't. Couldn't. For as the resolve swelled in him to do that very thing, he heard the gentle swish of grass being crumpled underfoot as someone approached from the opposite side of the rise.

Mom, Timmy thought with a sigh of relief, and wondered if she too would see this miraculous pocket of daylight and calm where there should be a storm.

But it wasn't his mother.

The man who came striding over the rise was longhaired and thickly built, his faded denim jeans ripped across the knees and trailing threads. He wore battered tan loafers, comfortable looking but tired and dying. A v-shaped patch of tangled black chest hair sprouted from the open neck of the man's navy shirt. He looked normal, except for one horrifying detail.

He had no face.

Beneath the brim of a dark blue baseball cap, there was nothing but a blank oval that twitched and shifted as if made of liquid. The flesh-colored surface darkened in places as if plagued by the memory of bruises and now and again, the suggestion of features—a dark eye, the twist of a smile—surfaced from the swimming skin. But otherwise, it was unfinished, a doll's face left to melt in the sun.

Timmy opened his mouth to speak, but the stranger spoke first, his words jovial and clear despite the absence of a mouth. "Hey there!" he said pleasantly. "You're Jodie's kid, right?"

Timmy frowned and backed up a step as the man continued to approach him. Darryl didn't seem perturbed by the faceless man, leading Timmy to believe they were not seeing the same thing.

"Yes. Who are you?" said a young voice behind Timmy, and he turned to see Darryl looking at him…no, not at him…looking through him to the stranger. Stricken, but feeling as though he had intruded on a conversation not meant for him, he stepped away so he could watch this bizarre interaction.

The stranger's eyes resolved themselves from the shimmering mass of his face— so blue they were almost white—then gone again. "I'm a friend of your uncle's. We're practically *best* friends!"

"Really?" said Darryl, sounding dubious.

"Sure. We chug a few beers every Friday night. Game of poker every other Thursday." He stepped forward until his shadow sprawled across the boy. "You ever play poker?"

"Yes, sir. Once. My daddy taught me before he left us."

The stranger nodded his sympathy. "Shit, that's hard. I feel for you kid. Really, I do. Can't be easy waitin' on a daddy that might not ever come back."

Darryl's eyes clouded with pain. "Yes, sir."

"Hey, c'mon," the man said, hunkering down next to the boy. "Don't be so down. If he didn't hang around, that's his loss, right? Besides, you got people—good people—looking out for you right here."

"Like who, sir?"

"Well, let's see…" The stranger's awful blank face turned to look out over the water at trees so green they were almost luminescent beneath the sun. "Well, me for one."

Darryl shrugged. "But I don't know you."

"Ah that's okay. I didn't know you either. Least until now. Heck, we're practically best friends now, right?"

"You smell like beer," Darryl said, a quaver in his voice.

Though it was not there for him to see, Timmy sensed the stranger's smile fade. He couldn't understand why Darryl, or the man, couldn't see him and why Darryl wasn't seeing the man's face, or lack of one. Were they ghosts? If so, then what did that make the version of Darryl they had seen on the bank with the pieces missing?

"Yeah, I knocked back a few before I came over. So what? One of these days you'll be tipping beers like your old man, I'm willing to bet."

"My daddy doesn't drink. At least he didn't while he was with us. He said it was evil."

"Well, shit and sugar fairies boy, your old man sounds like a real party animal." He threw his head back and laughed. It wasn't a kind sound, the echo even less so.

He reached into his shirt pocket and produced a crumpled cigarette. He set about straightening it, then paused and held it out to the boy seated next to him. "You want a puff?"

Darryl shook his head and reached for his notebook. He was obviously preparing to make a hasty exit. The stranger stopped him with a gesture, a dirty fingernail aimed at the little red square in the grass between them. "What's this? A diary?"

"No sir." Darryl made to retrieve the notebook, but the man snatched it up and switched it to the hand farther away from the boy.

"What have we here?" With one hand, he flipped through the pages with a soiled thumb, his other hand snapping open a Zippo lighter and bringing the flame to the tip of the crooked cigarette, jammed low between lips that weren't there.

Darryl looked crestfallen and stared at his submerged ankle as he muttered, "It's a story."

"A story, eh? Like a war story?"

"No. A love story."

"Aw shit!" the man said, coughing around his cigarette and chuckling. "You a little fairy boy?"

Darryl shrugged. "I don't know what that means."

"Sure you do. You like boys?"

"Yes, sir. Some of them."

The man slapped his knee, knocking the ash from his cigarette into the water. "Shit, I knew it!"

It was clear by the expression on the boy's face that he didn't know just what it was the man 'knew' and wanted to leave so bad it hurt. Timmy, still paralyzed by disbelief at where and how and possibly *when* he had found himself, felt a pang of sorrow for the boy and wished the stranger would leave him alone.

But the man stayed where he was and flipped a lock of chestnut-colored hair from the ghost of his eyes as his laugh grew hoarse, then died. "I knew a fairy boy like you once," he said. A mouth appeared in the skin-mask as he attempted to blow a smoke ring but only managed a mangled S before the breeze snatched it away. "Couple of years ago, back in college. He was like you, you know. Dressed real nice, spoke real good. Had no time for anyone he thought beneath him, if you'll excuse the pun, which meant pretty much everybody was beneath the sonofabitch. That cocksucker didn't get to me though. No sir. I fixed his goddamn wagon real good."

"I'd better go. Can I have my book?" Darryl withdrew his foot from the water. He braced his hands beneath him to lever himself up and that's when it happened.

Just as Darryl began to rise, the man, in one smoothly executed move, clenched the fist holding the cigarette and swept his arm hard beneath the boy's hands, dropping him hard on his back. Timmy heard the whoosh of the boy's breath as he lay confused and frightened. He saw the bobbing of the boy's Adam's apple as the fear registered. And then the man rose, his shadow once again draping itself over Darryl.

"Stop it! Leave him alone!" Timmy roared, but he felt as if he was locked inside a glass cage.

"Now why'd you have to go and get all impolite on me, huh? Weren't we having a good little chat, just the two of us? No women, no bitching, no bills, no bullshit. Just you and me having a fine time." His 'face' darkened. "What would your daddy think if he knew what you are? Or does he know? Are you queer because of him? Is that it? Shit, that's terrible. I mean, I feel sorry for you, man. I really do. No kid should have to deal with that shit. I mean, my father got drunk one time and tried to—"

Darryl ran. It happened that fast. One minute he was on his back, trembling like an upturned crab, and the next he was on his feet and running toward the trees.

And the stranger fell on him. To Timmy it seemed as if the man had hardly moved and yet he was there, lying across the area of flattened grass Darryl had occupied only a moment before, both hands wrapped around the boy's ankle, the cigarette forgotten and smoldering between them.

"Let me go!" Darryl cried and clawed at the grass. "Please, let me go!"

The stranger grunted and tugged the boy back toward him, flipped him over and struck him once across the face with his fist. It was enough. Darryl's cries faded to a whine, tears streaming down his face and scissoring through the dirt smudged there.

The man shuffled forward and sat down on the boy's legs, trapping him. Darryl regarded him with animal panic, subdued only by the threat of further violence.

"Aw Jesus," the stranger said as twin trails of blood began to run from the boy's nostrils. "Aw Jesus," he repeated, grabbing fistfuls of his long hair and tugging hard. "Look what you did. Look what you did," he said, over and over as if it was a spell to ward off consequences. "Look what you did. You're bleeding. You'll tell. You'll run and tell and they'll throw me in jail. All because you couldn't just be polite and sit and listen. No, you tried to run. You tried to run away and *look what you did!*"

"Please," Darryl sobbed beneath him.

A few feet away, Timmy wept too. He wanted to help, wanted to make this stop, somehow prevent what was going to happen because he knew, just *knew* in his heart and soul what was going to happen next.

He screamed then and looked away, knowing the scream wasn't entirely his own, aware his own vocalized pain was drowning out the anguished cry of the boy on the bank. Timmy saw the man's hands settling on both sides of the boy's neck and looked away. He moaned and fell to his knees on the edges of a killer's shadow as a sound like dry twigs snapping told him Darryl was dead.

13

A N ETERNITY PASSED before he looked up again. The killer stood there sobbing into his fist, but only for a moment. He quickly composed himself and set about tugging old rocks from where they had stood untouched for many years. He carried them to the inert body lying sprawled on the bank and stuffed the biggest ones under the boy's shirt and down his trousers. After wrenching Darryl's shirt into a crude knot to hold the rocks, he grabbed the boy's legs around the ankles. Darryl's head lolled sickeningly, the sightless eyes finding Timmy for the first time. Timmy felt sick, this new world of sunshine and murder seen through tears as he watched the killer step back into the water, the man's face swirling. He dragged the boy's body into the pond, held it in his arms for a moment, the water lapping at his waist, then let go and watched it sink, watched as bubbles broke the surface and the ripples fled.

Timmy wiped a sleeve across his eyes and sobbed, the tears hot with rage and horror. His temples throbbed. It hurt to think, to see, to bear witness to something so appallingly brutal. He knew he would never be the same again.

He looked up in time to see the stranger clambering onto the bank, his jeans darkened by the water, streams trickling from beneath the cuffs. He was weeping mud-colored tears, muttering beneath his breath, cussing and batting at the air over his head as he slipped and fell, then hurried to his feet. He almost forgot the book, but then turned and scooped it up and jammed it into his inside pocket. He looked around and, for one soul-freezing moment, his gaze found Timmy's but then continued to scan the surrounding area for signs that he'd been seen or that someone had heard the boy. Satisfied that he was alone, he cast one final glance back at the water before heading back toward the rise, his head bowed.

After a moment, Timmy got to his feet and moved toward the bank. A dewdrop of blood glistened on the sunbaked grass. A hush fell over the pond, so noticeable that Timmy looked up at the sky. A raindrop smacked him on the forehead, and he jumped, startled.

Something in the pond made a sucking sound and his gaze snapped down to where the surface of the water was starting to heave.

The air hummed. There came a noise like the sea heard in a conch shell and the hair rose on Timmy's arms. Lightning fractured the sky and normality returned with a sound like heavy sheets of glass shattering. The boy staggered back a step. The rushing sound grew louder.

And then day exploded in one deafening scream into night. And rain.

Timmy tottered forward. The rain hammered against his skull, soaking him. He almost lost his footing. He regained his balance and squinted into the thick dark. In the distance, someone called his name. Lightning strobed again; the shadows crouched around the pond flinched. Another cry, from somewhere behind him.

He turned and a figure rose in front of him. "It's all your fault," Mr. Marshall sobbed. He drew back his fist and a darkness darker than night itself swept itself on wings of sudden pain into Timmy's eyes and he felt the ground pull away from him. A moment of nothingness in which he almost convinced himself he had dreamed it all, despite the stars that coruscated behind his eyelids, and then an immense cold shocked him back into reality. He thrashed his arms and felt them move far too slowly for the weight of his panic. An attempt to scream earned him nothing but a mouthful of choking water and he gagged, convulsed, and tried to scream again. *Oh God help me I can't swim!* His mind felt as if it too were filling with water and suddenly, he ceased struggling, his throat closing, halting its fight against the dirty tide flowing through it. His heart thudded. One more breath. Water. Then a blanket of soothing whispers, a sheet of warmth draped over him and he no longer felt the pain of his lungs burning. It was as if he were feeling the pain in a separate body, a body he could ignore if he chose to.

And ignore it he did as he sank and drifted on waves of peace that carried him away. Until a sharp pain drove the resignation from his brain and his leg twitched, spasmed, and he was jerked from the panacea of death's reverie. His eyes fluttered open. Darkness, but darkness he could feel between his fingers. Another bite and his heart kicked. Agony. Water. Something was gnawing on his foot. A self-preserving panic like liquid fire swelled in him and he kicked, struggled, pushed himself up to where the water moved with purpose and rhythm, shifting to the sound of the storm.

More pain, needling between his toes, and his head broke water, panic rattling his skull as he drew a breath and went under once more. He struggled against the heaving water, his tongue numb, cottoned by the acrid taste of the fetid depths. The water fell below his neck and he sucked greedily at the air, aware for the first time that the storm vied for dominance with the sounds of human violence. Men yelled, a woman screamed, and someone called his name.

This time he stayed above water, his frantic paddling halting abruptly when his foot connected with something hard, something unmoving. He could stand and did so falteringly, his chest full of red-hot needles as the water shifted around him, trying to reclaim him. It rushed from his stomach, his lungs, his mind and he vomited, vomited until he felt as if his head would explode, then he staggered in the storm-induced current, his face raised to the rain.

A splash behind him. Timmy turned, blinking away tears, rain, pond water and trying to focus on something other than his own lingering blindness and trembling bones.

The Turtle Boy stood before him, unaffected by the tumultuous heaving of the water. He looked as he had when Pete and Timmy had found him, his face mottled and decayed. He wore a coat now and the coat moved. Timmy stepped back, the bank so preciously close and yet so far away.

"You saw it," Darryl croaked, the shoulders of his coat sprouting small heads that sniffed the air before withdrawing. "You stepped behind The Curtain and you saw what he did."

Somehow Timmy could hear him over the storm, over the churning of the water, though Darryl did not raise his voice to compete with them. He nodded, not trusting his voice.

"You don't know who did it. When you do, remember what you saw and let it change you. There is only time to let one of them pay for his crimes tonight."

"I don't understand!" Timmy felt dizzy, sick; he wanted to be home and warm, away from the madness this night had become, if it was really night at all.

"You will. *They'll* explain it to you."

"Who?"

"People like me. The people on The Stage."

Darryl swept past him and in the transient noon of lightning, he saw the coat was fashioned from a legion of huge, ugly turtles, their shells conjoined like a carapace around the boy's chest and back. Wizened beaks rose and fell, worm-like tongues testing the air as Darryl carried them toward the bank and the figures who fought upon it.

From here, Timmy could see his mother and Kim, huddled at the top of the rise, his mother's hand over Kim's face to keep her from seeing something. He followed their gaze to the two men wrestling each other in the dark.

Dad! Possessed by new resolve that numbed the flaring pain in his feet and the throbbing in his chest and throat, he thrashed to the bank and reached it the same time Darryl did. They both climbed over, both paused as the storm illuminated the sight of Wayne Marshall punching Timmy's father in the face—

Just like he punched Darryl before he killed him

—and stooped to retrieve something he'd dropped as the other man reeled back. Over the cannon roar of thunder, Timmy heard his mother scream his name and resisted the urge to look in her direction as he slipped, slid and flailed and finally tumbled to the ground between her and where his father was straightening and bracing himself for a bullet from the weapon in Wayne Marshall's hand.

.

14

IN THE STORM-LIGHT, Mr. Marshall grinned a death's head rictus, his skin pebbled with rain. He raised the gun. Timmy's father cradled his head in his arms and backed away.

Mr. Marshall pulled the trigger.

And nothing happened.

He jerked back his hand and roared at the gun, fury rippling through him. "*No, fuck you, NO!*"

He thrust the gun out, aimed it at Timmy's father's head and pulled the trigger.

Nothing.

Again and again and again, nothing but a series of dry snapping sounds.

"God*damn* you!"

"No!" Timmy yelled, then realized it hadn't come from his stricken throat at all. It was Darryl and his cry had not been one of protest. It had been a command.

And it was heeded.

The ground beneath Timmy's hands moved, separated into ragged patches of moving darkness, slick and repulsive against his skin. He jerked back and rose unsteadily, eyes fixed on the moving earth, waiting for the lightning to show him what he already knew.

The turtles. An army of them. All monstrous, all ancient. And all moving toward where his father had his arms held out to ward off the bullet that must surely be on its way.

"Timmy...son, stay back," he said, risking a quick glance at his son. "Just stay there."

"Dad!" This time Timmy knew from the pitiful croak that it was indeed his own voice.

He ran, halted, drowning again but in fear, confusion and the agony of uncertainty as the creatures Doctor Myers had introduced to his pond all those years ago trudged slowly but purposefully toward their prey.

"Darryl," Timmy cried, scorching his throat with the effort to be heard. Darryl looked toward him, the coat slowly shrugging itself off to join its brethren. "Darryl, please! Make them stop!"

Another shadow rose from the pond.

Timmy felt a nightmarish wave of disbelief wash over him. Even after all he'd been through, was *still* going through, he felt his mind tugging in far too many directions at once.

But there was not enough time to dwell on it.

He looked away from the new shadow and ran, skidding to the ground before his father. Darryl turned to look at him.

The turtles slowed.

"You'd die for your father?" Darryl asked, his voice little more than a gurgle.

"Yes!" Timmy screamed, without hesitation. "Yes! Leave him alone!"

"Why?"

"Because I *love* him. He's the best father in the world and I love him. You can't take him away from me. *Please!*"

"Maybe he deserves to die."

"Don't *say* that. He doesn't! I *swear* he doesn't!"

The storm itself seemed to hold its breath as Darryl stared and the impatience of the turtle army stretched the air taut.

A gentle pulse of lightning broke the stasis.

Darryl turned to regard the shadow standing in the water next to him. Pointing to Mr. Marshall, he asked the same question: "Would *you* die for *him?*"

Even Mr. Marshall seemed intent on the answer the shadow would give.

But it said nothing. Instead, it gave a gentle shake of its head.

"No!" Wayne cried as Darryl turned back to face him.

Slowly, Timmy's father lowered his hands and after a moment in which he realized Wayne Marshall's attention was elsewhere, he moved away into the shadows of the pines, his face a pale blur of horror as he saw what had his neighbor's attention.

Darryl turned back to watch the turtles advance. The first of them found Mr. Marshall's leg and after a moment of stunned disgust, he aimed his pistol downward and, in his panic, tried the weapon again.

This time the gun fired.

A deafening roar and the gun let loose a round that took most of Mr. Marshall's foot away with it. He shrieked and dropped to the ground, then realized his folly and scuttled backward on his hands. The dark tide moved steadily forward.

Timmy's father burst from his hiding place and ran the long way around the pond, through the pines, the marsh and along the high bank until he appeared through the weeds on the far side of the rise. His wife released Kim at last and ran to him.

Multi-colored lights lit the sky in the distance, back near the houses. Timmy guessed the police had arrived and were now searching for the woman who had summoned them. He silently begged them to hurry.

A guttural scream was all that could be heard from the shadows as the tide of turtles progressed ever onward and engulfed their victim.

A single flicker of lightning lit the face of the shadow in the water and Timmy felt a jolt of shock.

The dead and bloated face staring back at him was Pete's.

Oh God...

Someone grabbed Timmy's shoulder and spun him roughly around. He looked up into the frightened face of his father, noticed his swollen eye and crushed nose, and almost wept again, but there was no time. The sirens were growing louder, drowning out the shrieks and snapping sounds from beneath the pines. Timmy let himself be led and almost didn't feel Kim's hand slipping into his own. He smiled at her, but it was an empty gesture. There was nothing to be cheerful about and, head afire with unanswered questions, he looked over his shoulder as they descended the rise as one huddled, broken mass. Pete was gone. The earth still crawled and among the seething shadows The Turtle Boy stood, unsmiling in his victory.

15

TIMMY SLEPT FOR DAYS AFTERWARD, speaking only to his parents and Kim and occasionally a police officer who tried his best to look positive. Timmy saw the horror in the man's eyes, a horror that began on a warm sunny morning at the start of summer.

What he learned, he learned from his father, the papers and Kim who in turn had heard it from her own parents—apparently too shocked to be discreet in their gossiping.

They had pulled three bodies out of the pond. One was a young boy, little more than a skeleton cocooned in algae. According to the medical examiner's report, he had been there for some time and had died as a result of a broken neck, sustained it was assumed, by a fall from an old tire swing that had hung for a brief time above the pond back in the late sixties. They had identified the body as Darryl Gaines, nephew of the second decedent, Wayne Marshall. Apparently,

Marshall's nephew had visited him back in 1967 while his mother was being treated for drug abuse. Marshall was drinking in his backyard with friends and poking fun at the boy (this, from Geoff Keeler, an ex-buddy of Wayne's) and the kid had run off in a sulk. They'd never seen him again. Divers had searched the pond and come up empty ("apart from some big <bleepin> turtles" one of them stated on the news, obviously relishing the attention of the camera). Shortly after, Darryl's mother, Joanne Gaines was institutionalized. She committed suicide a month later.

The third body filled Timmy with a wave of grief he was afraid would never leave him. Every time he stared up at his bedroom ceiling; every time he glanced at a comic book or thought about the red clay in Patterson's field, he saw Pete's face.

Pete had never made it to summer camp. His body had shown signs of chronic physical abuse, culminating in a broken neck sustained—per the evidence obtained from the Marshall house—from a fall against the edge of a marble fireplace. It was assumed Wayne Marshall had killed his son by accident, in a fit of alcohol-fueled rage.

Panicked, Wayne decided to dump his son's body in the pond (perhaps so he could claim later that the boy had run away) and was readying himself to do so when Timmy's father arrived on the scene.

"I just stood looking at him," Timmy's father said. "I couldn't believe what I was seeing. Wayne, with Pete in his arms...I didn't want to believe he was dead, couldn't believe Wayne would kill his own son. I watched him lay the boy down on the grass. That's when he pulled the gun on me. That's when I saw his eyes and knew he was lost. Jesus, I should have *known*, should have done something sooner."

Timmy only smiled through the tears when he thought of what Darryl's turtles might have done to Wayne Marshall.

Wayne Marshall, the faceless man Timmy had seen at the pond, murdering his nephew and leaving him beneath the water to feed the turtles.

The visitors came and went, attempted to soothe Timmy with words he couldn't hear and through it all, through the mindless passage of feverish recollection and the debilitating agony of loss, The Turtle Boy's words returned to him again and again, nagging at him and begging to be decoded: You don't know who did it. *When you do, remember what you saw and let it change you.*

Maybe he deserves to die.

Three weeks later, they filled in the pond. They'd been trying for years but somehow mechanical difficulties had always kept them away. Timmy thought he now knew what had caused those problems.

16

SUMMER ENDED, AND AS PER THE RULES of the seasons in Ohio, there was no subtle ushering out of the warmth; the weather dropped in temperature and the earth darkened on the very day the calendar page turned.

Spurning all attempts his father made at trying to come up with something fun for them to do on what might be the last Saturday of good weather for quite some time, Timmy took a walk.

Fall was already setting up camp on the horizon, prospecting for leaves to burn and painting the sky with colors from a bruised pallet.

He wanted to forget but knew that would never happen.

There were three reasons why the fear would always be with him, dogging his every step and making stalkers out of the slightest shadows.

First, the reporters. In the months since Pete's and Mr. Marshall's deaths, the newspapers had played up the ghost angle, delighting in the idea that an eleven-year-old boy had helped solve a murder through an alleged conference with the dead. There were phone calls, insistent and irritating, from jocular voices proclaiming their entitlement to Timmy's story.

They were ignored.

But this only led to speculation, and Timmy's face ended up in the local newspapers, topped with giant bold lettering that read:

11-YEAR-OLD BOY RESURRECTS THE DEAD, SOLVES MURDER!

Then the curiosity seekers started showing up, some of them from the media, most of them just regular folk. Their neediness frightened the boy. *We just want to touch him*, they said. Others wept and begged his mother to *let the boy see if he can bring my little Davey/Suzy/Alex/Ricky/Sheri back.* And they were still coming to the house, though not as much as they had in the beginning.

The second reason was that even if Timmy managed to dismiss the calls, the desperate pleas of strangers, the newspaper reports, and the occasional mention of his name on the television, there were still the nightmares. Vivid, brutal, and unflinching. In his dreams, he saw everything, all the things he had been able to look away from in real life. All the things he had been able to run from.

Every night, he drowned and ended up behind what Darryl had called 'The Curtain.' In the waking hours, the name stayed with him, conjuring images in Timmy's mind of a tattered black veil drawn wide across a crumbling stage. He imagined a whole host of the dead crouching behind it, waiting for their chance to come back, to find their own killers. And perhaps they would. Perhaps also they would only be successful if they had someone to draw strength from, as Timmy was sure Darryl Gaines had drawn strength from him and Pete.

Or perhaps it was over.

Believing that required the most effort.

Because the final reason, the last barrier stopping him from releasing the dread and shaking off the skeins of clambering horror was the recollection of something else The Turtle Boy had said: *You don't know who did it. When you do, remember what you saw and let it change you.* He had mulled over this every day and every night since the discovery of the bodies. It would have been simpler to forget had he not realized something about the murders, something that came back to him weeks later—Wayne Marshall was Darryl's uncle. The story had it that Darryl had been visiting his uncle and that's why he was there in the first place. But Timmy had been there, however it had happened, standing on the bank of the pond when the big man had come strolling over the rise. Among the things he'd said had been *I'm a friend of your uncle's. We're practically best friends!* Which meant Darryl's murderer had not been his uncle.

But every time it got this far in Timmy's head, heavy black pain descended like a caul over him and he had to stop and think of nothing until it went away. It was too much. Maybe in the years to come it would make sense. For now, it would hang like an old coat in a closet, always there but seldom worn.

Maybe he deserves to die.

His walk took him back to the pond, to where bulldozers stood like slumbering monsters next to a smoothened oval of dirt. They'd drained the pond and ripped away the banks. The telltale signs of man were everywhere now, the animals quiet. Despite his relief at having the dark water gone, Timmy couldn't help the twinge of sadness he felt at having the good memories buried beneath that hard-packed dirt, too. All around him the land was changing, becoming unfamiliar.

He sighed, dug his hands in his pockets and walked on, unsure where he was heading until he was standing staring down at the railroad tracks. A cold breeze ran invisible fingers across his skin, and he shivered. A quick glance in both directions showed the tracks were deserted. No trains, no funny tireless cars with flashing yellow beacons.

School would begin soon, and he hoped it would be the distraction he needed from the crawling sensation he had been forced to live with, the sense of always being watched, of never being alone.

It'll pass, son, his father had told him, *I promise.*

Timmy prayed that was true.

Because even now, with not a soul around, he could feel it: a slight thrumming, as of a train coming, the air growing colder still, the sky appearing to brood and twist, the hiss of the wind through the tall grass on either side of the rails.

And a droning, faint at first.

A droning. Growing.

Like a machine. Or an engine.

Pete's voice then, disgruntled, whispering on the wind: *They were stupid to ride that close to the train anyway.*

Not an engine.

Muscles stiffening, Timmy drew his hands out of his pockets, held his hands by his sides. He felt his knees bend slightly and knew his body had decided to run, seemingly commanded by the small fraction of unpanicked mind that remained. He looked to the right. Nothing but empty track, winding off out of sight around a bramble-edged bend.

He looked to the left.

The wind rose, carrying the stench of death to him and he felt his heart hammer against his ribcage. A child, limping, trying to prevent himself from toppling over, all his energy focused on keeping the mangled dirt bike—and himself—upright.

I wish that kid hadn't been killed up there.

The bike, sputtered, growled, whined. Or perhaps it was Danny Richards making the awful sounds—Timmy couldn't tell.

The child's bisected mouth dropped open, teeth missing, as he lurched forward, the weight of the bike threatening to drag him down and Timmy bolted, ran for his life. The wind followed him, drowning out his own screams, thwarting his attempts to deafen the mournful wail coming from the stitched-together boy hobbling along the railroad tracks.

"*Where's my sissssssterrrrr?*"

Timmy stopped for breath by the memory of the pond. He could still see the boy, a distant figure lurching along the tracks—a pale, bruised shape against the dark green grass.

Something's wrong, something's broken. Timmy knew it then as if it had been delivered in a hammer-strike blow to the side of his head. He sobbed at the realization that the They Darryl had mentioned, the They who would show him what he needed to learn, were the dead. He would see them now. Again and again.

Everywhere.

And there was a truth he had missed, a truth he was not yet ready—not yet able—to figure out on his own. All that was left were questions:

Why did he want to hurt Dad?

Why did he ask me if I'd die for him?

Why did he say maybe he deserved to die?

As he straightened, struggling not to weep at the thought of what might yet lay ahead of him, he flinched so hard his neck cracked, a cold sheet of pain spreading over his skull.

A voice that might have been the breeze.

A whisper that might have been the trees.

And a face that peered over his right shoulder, grinning.

Timmy choked on a scream.

"*Mine, now,*" said Mr. Marshall.

The Delaw

11-YEAR-OLD BOY RES

Local boy Timmy Quinn (11) was in a state of shock yesterday as police and paramedics descended on the Quinn home after the discovery of two bodies in the nearby Myers Pond. The identities of the deceased have not yet been confirmed, but at least one is thought to be Darryl Gaines, a child who went missing in the area in 1962.

But perhaps the strangest element in the case is how the bodies were discovered in the first place. Although the Quinn

for comment, police say Timmy Quinn told them he was "visited by the ghost of the Gaines boy", which led him to Myers Pond and the gruesome discovery.

According to Sheriff Hancock, Timmy was "visibly distraught" and that there are circumstances surrounding the case which "will be made available to the press over the coming days". Although typically tight-lipped on the details, we have been able to glean a few facts from neighbors who were on the scene.

The Timmy Quinn series

Book 1: *The Turtle Boy*

Book 2: *The Hides*

Book 3: *Vessels*

Book 4: *Peregrine's Tale*

Book 5: Nemesis: *The Death of Timmy Quinn*

ABOUT THE AUTHOR

Hailed by <u>Booklist</u> as "one of the most clever and original talents in contemporary horror," Kealan Patrick Burke was born and raised in Ireland and emigrated to the United States a few weeks before 9/11. Since then, he has written five novels, among them the popular southern gothic slasher *Kin* and over two hundred short stories and novellas, including *Sour Candy* and *The House on Abigail Lane*, both of which have been optioned for film.

A five-time Bram Stoker Award-nominee, Burke won the award in 2005 for his coming-of-age novella *The Turtle Boy*, the first book in the acclaimed Timmy Quinn series.

As editor, he helmed the anthologies *Night Visions 12*, *Taverns of the Dead*, and *Quietly Now*, a tribute anthology to one of Burke's influences, the late Charles L. Grant.

Most recently, he adapted his work to comic book format for four volumes of John Carpenter's *Tales for a Halloween Night* series of anthologies and contributed a short story to Mike Mignola and Christopher Golden's *Hellboy: An Assortment of Horrors*. He is currently at work on a new novel, *Mr. Stitch*.

Kealan is represented by Merrilee Heifetz at Writers House and Kassie Evashevski at Anonymous Content.

He lives in an unhaunted house in Ohio with a Scooby Doo lookalike rescue named Red.

You can find him on the web at kealanpatrickburke.com or on Twitter @kealanburke

Printed in Great Britain
by Amazon